Don't Say Good Bye Just Say *See You!*

Patricia A. Brill, PhD

Illustrated by Curt Walstead

functional
fitness
L.L.C.

Dedication

This book is dedicated in loving memory to my mother
Mary Jean Brill who lost her battle with cancer. She would
never say "Good Bye." She would just say "See You!" To my mother,
Good Bye was something you would say to someone you may not
see again. See You meant that sometime in the future
she would see us again.

While in Hospice, with her family standing around her,
she drew her last breath, and whispered, "See You!"

Hello All—

The story I am about to tell you is about my best friend Boxster.

TURBO

Boxster was always there for me: sharing his food after I gulped down all of mine; bailing me out when I was a bad dog; and supporting me twice when I had cancerous moles removed from my legs and back. After my first surgery, the nurses called me Frankendog! I was scared, but Boxster was always with me.

Together, Boxster and I faced many challenges. But when we learned Boxster had cancer, we knew this would be our biggest challenge of all. Boxster developed a large tumor between his hip bones. The vet, who was called Dr. Larry, said the tumor was rapidly growing so he couldn't operate to remove it.

My best friend was in pain. He had difficulty walking, and lost his appetite. He could no longer drag his favorite bed out the doggie door. But worse of all he lost his desire to run and jump and spin and play. Boxster was ready to go to heaven, but I wasn't ready to say Good Bye.

I want you to know that sometimes bad things happen to people we love, but the best you can do for them is to be there whenever they need you; even though they might not know they need you. I understand what happened to Boxster was not his fault, but I still feel angry and sad over the loss of my best friend. With time his loss will get easier, but his memory will never fade.

Love,

Turbo

"Boxster look!" exclaimed Turbo. "There's a squirrel. Let's chase it."

"I can't chase them anymore" sighed Boxster. "My hip hurts to much to even run and jump and spin and play."

"I don't feel very well," said Boxster. "Remember Turb when you didn't want to eat or play with your toys. Then we found out you had cancer? Well I feel the same way."

"Well we are going to see Dr, Larry the Vet right away"
demanded Turbo. "Dr. Larry helped me so he can help you as well."

"He will put you up on the shiny, cold bed and run some
tests to find out exactly what is wrong with you. But don't worry
Boxster," assured Turbo, "the bed isn't as cold as it looks." Boxster
smiled.

With his nose pressed against the glass, Turbo sat patiently watching Boxster as Dr. Larry ran several tests, including an ultrasound.

When Dr. Larry was finished running the tests, he turned to Turbo and said, "The ultrasound showed that Boxster has a tumor growing between his hip bones. The tumor is causing him to limp and not feel very well. Because the tumor is so large and growing so fast, it is too late to operate to remove it. There is nothing else we can do but keep him comfortable and let him know he is loved until he dies."

Turbo bolted to the table. "Oh Boxster" said Turbo. "I don't know what to say."

"You don't have to say anything" said Boxster. "Just being here with me is all I need."

"Boxster, I'm sad. I don't want you to die."

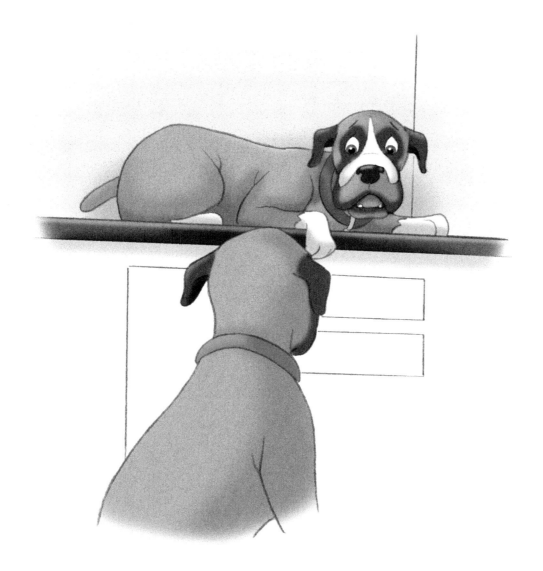

"It's okay to be sad. It's even okay to be mad. But I want you to realize that when I die I will finally be out of pain. My cancer will be gone; I won't limp anymore; my appetite will be back; and I will be able to play with all the other dogs in heaven. In time your sadness will ease and you will be able to remember all the happy times we shared."

"I'm scared I'll be all alone. Will I ever see you again?" asked Turbo.

"Yes," assured Boxster, "When it is time. But until then I want you to find a new best friend so you can run and jump and spin and play. Making a new friend will never take anything away from what we had together. Just know that I will be happy if you are happy. You were such a great friend to me. Other dogs need a friend like you. Just tell them about me every once in a while and how I always kept you from being a bad dog."

Boxster crawled into his favorite doggie bed. Turbo snuggled
in tight next to him, placing his head across his back. Tears rolled
down his fur. "I don't want to die alone" whispered Boxster. "Don't

worry" said Turbo, "I'll be right here with you. You were always there for me so now it is my time to be there for you."

"Thanks for being with me through all of this" said Boxster. "You're welcome" said Turbo, "That's what best friends are for." Boxster sighed. "Turb I'm tired. I'm going to heaven now."

"But Boxster" cried Turbo. "I'm not ready to say good bye."

"Don't say Good Bye," replied Boxster. "Just say See You!"

"Why See You?" asked Turbo in puzzlement.

Boxster perked his head up a little and said, "Because Good Bye is something you say to someone you may not see again. See You means that sometime in the future we will see each other again. It might be a short while, or it might be a long time. But never the less, we will see each other again!"

"What if for some reason you can't say See You?" asked Turbo.

"Then right before I'm ready to go to heaven, I will wiggle my tail. That will be my way of saying, See You."

"Boxster," asked Turbo. "When I die will you be there to greet me?"

"You bet!" exclaimed Boxster. "I'll be there along with our angels and all the other humans and dogs we knew who died before us. And when we meet again we will know that nothing will ever separate us again. We'll be able to run and jump and spin and play in Heaven's big back yard all day!"

Boxster closed his eyes, wiggled his tail, and quietly went to heaven. Turbo whispered "See you."

Dear Boxster:

If we could have just one more day to run and jump and spin and play. To eat more treats and bask in the sun, to bolt out the doggie door and go for a run.

If I could have just one more day to ask my angels what words to say. To let you know how much I care, you were my best friend - You were always there.

If I could have just one more day, I'd even let you have your way!

I will miss you always.

Love, Turbo

∾

ISBN-13: 978-0-9815551-6-4 (Hardcover)
ISBN-13: 978-0-9815551-7-1 (Paperback)

Printed in the U.S.A.

Illustrated by Curt Walstead

Book design by DesignForBooks.com

CPSIA information can be obtained
at www.ICGtesting.com
Printed in the USA
LVOW05s1913261116
514570LV00001B/1/P